THE MUMMY WORE COMBAT BOOTS

ELISE ABRAM

EMSA
PUBLISHING

The Mummy Wore Combat Boots
Copyright © 2012 by Elise Abram
Copyright © 2014 by Elise Abram
Copyright © 2017 by Elise Abram

Published by EMSA Publishing 2017
Thornhill, Ontario, Canada

The final approval for this literary material is granted by the author.

Third printing
This is a work of fiction. Any similarity between the characters and situations within its pages and places or persons, living or dead, is unintentional and coincidental.

Printing History
First Edition: October 2012
Second Edition: August 2014 with *Throwaway Child*
Third Edition: August 2017

PUBLISHED BY EMSA PUBLISHING
http://emsapublishing.com

The Mummy Wore Combat Boots is printed in Georgia.

Credits: Cover font: Norse by Joël Carrouché
Interior font: Georgia
Cover art: "Ancient stone carved Egyptian hieroglyphs in Egypt" ID 149030102 ©Przemyslaw Skibinski | Shutterstock.com
Cover design: Elise Abram

ALSO BY ELISE ABRAM

The Nexus and Other Stories
The New Recruit
I Was, Am, Will Be Alice
The Revenant: A YA Paranormal Thriller with
Zombies
Phase Shift
Throwaway Child

1

Mummies are the stuff of legends. The ancient Egyptians practiced the art of mummification in order to preserve the body for the afterlife. The Victorians were fascinated by them and hosted mummy unwrapping parties. For these events, mummies were shipped to England and literally unwrapped, so the elite might marvel at the remains. The obsession with all things Egyptian abroad led to the creation of a mummy trade in Egypt. To fuel the demand for this morbid industry, ordinary graves were robbed, the poor unfortunates made into pharonic knockoffs in order to turn a fast buck with unsuspecting tourists.

If I were there, I like to think I would have known. That they were fakes, I mean. My name is Palmer Richardson. I teach archaeology at the University of Toronto in Ontario, Canada. My specialty is forensic anthropology. I'm like those guys you see on television who work alongside the police to identify murder victims, especially when all that's left are the bones. Virtually everything a person does in life leaves its mark on the bones.

Things like sex, age, diet, physical activity—it's all there, written in the bones. The trick is in learning how to read the signs.

I was contacted by Suzanne Pascoe, the Egyptology curator at the Royal Ontario Museum, when several unidentified mummies turned up during its most recent revitalization. The ROM's undergone many renovations since it opened almost a century ago. While it's regrettable, it stands to reason that some paperwork is bound to get lost in the shuffle. The situation was unacceptable, as far as Suzanne was concerned, and she made it her personal mission to catalogue each and every one of the unidentified mummies in the museum's collection. My job was to help dot the I's and cross the T's to fill in the gaps in the paperwork and possibly identify the remains. To aid us in our quest, Suzanne had convinced the hospital to schedule overnight X-ray and CT-scans, in a sort of virtual mummy unwrapping. The invitation to get up close and personal with a mummy doesn't happen often in one's career. Wild horses couldn't have kept me away from the opportunity, even though my wife wasn't exactly tickled pink at the prospect. You see, Suzanne's my ex-girl. She also happens to be a merciless flirt, especially where I'm concerned. I dumped Suzanne years ago. When I was with her, I never knew if she ever really considered me her partner, or just a serial one night stand. As corny as it sounds, my wife's my soul mate. Trust me: she has nothing to worry about.

The mummy on deck for X-rays was called Rahotep. A few technicians helped me lift him onto the table so we could shoot some film. Rahotep's mummy was enclosed in a cast-like,

6

cartonnage shell on which had been drawn a series of brightly-coloured glyphs in neat, vertical rows. Though I wasn't up on my ancient Egyptian, I was still able to pick out symbols for "warrior" and "prince", and for "blessed" and "honoured". Where my ancient Egyptian failed, Suzanne filled in the blanks. She leaned over Rahotep's linen and plaster sarcophagus and reached around me to point out the symbols. As she spoke I was enveloped in a haze of her perfume. Her scent was sweet and distantly floral. It brought back a slew of memories—not all of them disagreeable—in a dizzying flood.

"These symbols tell a narrative, a story of how Rahotep made a pilgrimage to Thebes to pay homage to Amun-Ra in the time of Amenhotep IV." She traced the symbols with a gloved finger as she spoke. "And over here?" She stepped around me, allowing a hand to rest briefly on the small of my back and trailing across it before moving on. My body shivered, welcoming her touch as my brain screamed in anger at the violation. Remember who you're with and why you're here, I scolded myself, even as I reasoned that some bodily responses were as autonomic as the beat of a heart.

"There's an account of his family's holdings. How much land they owned, their possessions, and the like." She continued to read from the list. Very interesting, even if it was uncomfortable for our proximity. "Strange though," she said distractedly, as she caressed a conglomeration of glyphs near Rahotep's left thigh, "the job looks rushed here, sloppy," as if she were noticing it for the first time.

"We found similar glyphs documented online," she continued, "almost like his handlers chose from stock text, like they chose two sayings from column A and three from column B and that's what they wrote." She looked from Rahotep back to me and smiled. The look lasted way too long, if you ask me. She had smoky eyes. I'd forgotten how alluring they were.

"Okay on your end, Paulie?" I hated that name, "Paulie". It was a pet name, residual of our old relationship. It was okay back then, cute, even. Now it made my skin crawl to hear it which had a sobering effect. This was Suzanne at my side, amorous, judgmental, (and in all likelihood, promiscuous) Suzanne. I was married to my wife, and happily at that.

I grunted something to indicate I was— ready, I mean—and along with a few technicians, managed to give Rahotep the old heave-ho and turn him over.

2

When the X-rays were done, Suzanne and I rushed the mummy to his CT-scan. Her demeanour had cooled considerably, probably in response to the cold front I was giving her. We kept our distance and watched as the scanner took pictures through his body in thin slices only millimetres thick, as if the machine were carving digital pot roast.

After that, we waited for the preliminary results.

"Our guy had fillings in his teeth," we were told by one of the technicians. He held the celluloid up to the light. "Here, and here," he said stabbing at the film with his forefinger. "They're so-called 'composite' fillings. White fillings."

The evidence was faint, but nevertheless there. "But composite fillings have only been around for twenty or so years," I said. "So...Rahotep's a fake?"

"So much for living under Amenhotep's reign," Suzanne said.

"So who's inside the bandages?" I asked.

"Well, he's male," said the technician. "Young. Just under six feet."

"How the hell did something like that find its way into my collection?" Suzanne asked.

"Wait," said the technician, "there's more. The young man died from a blow to the head. There's a fracture to the occipital lobe."

"Blunt force trauma?" I asked.

"Hard to tell from the pictures, but I'd say so, yeah."

"Have the police been notified yet?"

The technician shook his head. "I thought I'd break the news to you guys first."

Suzanne looked faint. All the blood had drained from her face, which made the thick layer of makeup she'd applied in spite of the hour look even thicker. She looked like a corpse that had walked away from a funeral home moments before the viewing.

As a forensic anthropologist, I sometimes freelance for the Metropolitan Toronto Police Service when I'm needed. When I heard the police needed to be notified, I decided to do the honours. I took out my cell and speed-dialed Detective Constable Michael Crestwood, my contact at the police department. "Blunt force trauma to the occipital lobe?" I said as I waited for the phone to dial. "A mummification in the Egyptian tradition? Rahotep, or whoever he is, was murdered."

3

I'd woken Crestwood from an early morning sleep. He met me at the front entrance of the hospital within an hour of my call, wearing track pants and a heavy parka. "Dr. Richardson," he said, stoically.

"Detective Crestwood," I countered. I filled him in on the situation on our way to the morgue— we'd moved Rahotep about a half hour before Crestwood arrived to make way for patients that were still breathing. We traversed the distance in silence, choosing to stare at the numbers above the door inside the elevator, rather than each other, which was unusual. It's been my experience that Crestwood's usually quite talkative, happy to regale anyone within listening distance about last night's sports scores or the specifics of the latest case he's closed. My guess was that on that particular night, on some level, Crestwood was still sleeping.

Crestwood gloved up and spent all of about a minute taking in the situation, which was fair, seeing as the poor guy *was* encased in a full-body cast. "Mummified, huh?" Crestwood finally said.

"Do we have permission to unwrap him, Officer?" asked the coroner. He looked barely out of high school.

"What do you say, Richardson?" Crestwood asked me.

"Suzanne said the drawings on the cartonnage had already been documented, so why not? Go for it."

We turned the mummy over and used scissors to cut through the back of the cartonnage casing and gently pried it open in order to preserve any trace evidence it might contain, things like hair or skin cells, or maybe even the fingerprints of the person who had created it. I wondered aloud if a handwriting analyst wouldn't be able to match paintings on the decorated mummy casing to everyday handwriting. Crestwood shrugged his response.

When, at last, the mummy had been revealed, I felt almost giddy. I watched as the face of a young man with chestnut hair and weak chin was revealed. His skin had the appearance of leather, thick and dark, detailing delicate, Caucasoid features. His lips had pulled into an accidental sneer, revealing widely-spaced, ivory teeth. I helped the coroner roll the linen bandages as they were pulled from the body. The boy we called Rahotep's chest was sunken. Though he appeared slim, his body fat would have rendered his belly soft and yielding in life. His chest was smooth and hairless, save for small patches of down on his pecs and under his arms. His legs seemed only slightly more muscular than the rest of his body, as might be expected if his only exercise was the occasional bout on a skateboard. The only distinguishing mark on his body was on his left bicep, a tattoo of an asp, green and scaly with crimson eyes, a single pearl of venom precariously positioned at the tip of an exaggerated fang. They're starting young these days, I thought, but then I remembered that I hadn't been that much older when I'd gotten my own tattoo, a skeleton (for obvious reasons) wearing a fedora (for reasons to which I'm not privy while sober), on my right pec. A bunch of us grad students got together and went on a bender after successfully defending our theses, a bender the likes of which I'd never before seen, nor have I ever cared to see since. Each of us came away from that night with a tattoo that was apparently representative of our specialties. Needless to say, I've been somewhat of a teetotaler ever since. I suppose I could have it removed, but the guy's grown on me. Besides, my wife thinks it's cute. Says it's my personal oxymoron, representing what I do, but not who I am. Insists she just can't picture someone with my personality walking into a tattoo parlour and ordering up a tattoo.

"He's just a baby," said the coroner, unable to see the irony in a statement that would have been just as fit had it been uttered as he looked at his own reflection.

"Can you get prints?" Crestwood asked.

The coroner tried to lift the boy's hand to bend it at the elbow, but the joint was immovable. Instead, he squatted to bring his eyes level with the hand as it rested on the autopsy table. Using a magnifying glass, he studied the fingertips. "I don't see why not," he finally said.

"Do that then. Get some prints," Crestwood demanded. "Get a shot of the tattoo, as well. And dental records, too. There are X-rays of this boy's

mouth in someone's dental office. Let's find them."
He rubbed his forehead with the back of his hand.
"What do *you* want to know, Richardson?" he
asked me.

I thought about his question for a moment.
What *did* I need in order to find out what had
happened to this poor boy? "Skin samples,
maybe?" I said, thinking aloud. "See if we can see
what they used to embalm him."

The coroner raised his surgical mask and
nodded in agreement. He positioned his scalpel
and cut three incisions, two from either shoulder
that met at the boy's sternum and then one down
the centre of his chest and belly. He appeared to
have some difficulty cutting through the tough,
leathery epidermis and adopted a sawing motion
as he worked.

"And the linen. Check for thread count and
material. And if you can get a decent picture of his
face without the wrappings, that might be good for
identification, too." I watched from a distance as
the coroner drew back the skin and removed the
sternum.

"You said this guy was mummified in true
Egyptian fashion, no?" asked the coroner.

"Yeah. Why?" asked Crestwood.

"Correct me if I'm wrong, but didn't the
Egyptians remove all of the internal organs?"

"They did," I told him, "They were
preserved in canopic jars, small effigy containers
representing various deities, or they wrapped them
in linens and stored them in the body cavity." The
coroner glared at me, as if what I was describing
was even more horrific than the task he was in the
process of completing. "Why do you ask?"

"'Cause this one's still got his heart," the coroner said.

"So the reproduction's only external, then," said Crestwood.

"Not exactly," I said. "The heart's often the only organ to be left behind. It was thought the soul would need it in the afterlife." I waited while he removed the heart, weighed it, and set it aside. "The cat-scan indicated his brain's been removed. Bones in the nasal passage are shattered," I told him.

"Body cavity's stuffed with..." the coroner reached in and removed a handful of a brown, mossy substance, "saw dust?"

I nodded. "They stuffed the body with sawdust or linens or other materials, plant matter and such, to help it keep its lifelike shape. Can we test that, too? If there's pollen or something else mixed in, it might help us to identify where it came from."

Crestwood began to say his goodbyes, but the coroner interrupted. "Uh, gentlemen?" he said. We turned to see him holding up a small package, neatly wrapped in linens. The coroner questioned us with his eyes, the only part of his face that was visible behind his mask.

"Internal organs," I told him. "Remember? Instead of canopic jars."

He tittered nervously and began stacking the packages beside the heart as he withdrew them from the body.

4

While I waited for the tox screen to come back, I got to work on the facial reconstruction.   There are certain landmarks on the skull that are unique to a person, things like the distance between the eyes and depth of eye sockets, or the angle of the jaw-line, or the shape of the chin. I used the CT rendering of the skull to feed these and other measurements into facial reconstruction software, printed out the results, and faxed them to Crestwood.

5

"Your reconstruction was bang on," Crestwood told me over the phone two days later. "We've identified the vic as Jason Hargrove, seventeen. Dental records confirm it. Went missing just over three months ago. Notified the parents last night."

"Any suspects?" I wondered.

"Not the parents, at least, not at this point. The casing still needs to be looked at with a fine-toothed comb, which will take a while.

"The lab results are back," he added. "The linen is simple cheesecloth that can be purchased quite inexpensively at any fabric store. It's impregnated with some kind of waxy resin that has beeswax as one of its chief ingredients. Cotton fibers.

"The tox report shows large amounts of sodium bicarbonate, sodium carbonate, sodium chloride, and sodium sulfate—"

"Natron," I told him.

"Come again?"

"Natron. It's what the Egyptians used as a desiccant to dry out the tissue."

"There are also traces of palm and cedar oils—"

"Used to keep the skin supple."

"There was nothing particularly interesting about the wood fibers pulled from the body cavity. Sorry about that."

"So we need to find a local supplier for palm and cedar oils, as well as one for natron," I said, "There can't be too many in the city."

"Unless they purchased it online. Then it could have come from anywhere in the world. Even if you found a supplier, if they used an anonymous IP address, you're shit out of luck, my friend.

"I'm heading over to the high school now to question the admin. You're welcome to come along for the ride if you'd like."

Sometimes I think I've missed my calling in life, that I should have pursued a career in criminology. I grew up on a steady diet of cop shows, watched them evolve during prime-time from corny to gritty and then settle (more recently) in the graphically morbid, but then I think about Crestwood and the stories he's told. Dodging accusations of unfair marking tactics and setting what I've been told are uncompassionate deadlines seems much tamer than dodging bullets and avoiding fist-fights with panicked perps, no matter how you slice it.

I agreed to meet Crestwood in the foyer of the school in an hour.

6

The city of Toronto has some schools that are architecturally regal, some of which hearken back almost a century. The prim, cut-stone foundations, sedate brick facades, and medieval turrets are throwbacks to a time when schools were institutions of learning, rather than storehouses for wayward youths to pass the time until they journeyed to adulthood through happenstance. When I arrived at Hargrove's school, I had to wade through a cohort of teens congregating in and around the school's entryway. Some students hovered while smoking on the sidewalk in front of the school, while others loitered on the front lawn, clouds of breath as white as smoke in the brisk, mid-winter air. The foyer was packed with underdressed teens speaking on cell phones or listening to rap music, ear buds permanently implanted in their aural canals. Standing out in the crowd was Crestwood, nervously jangling the change in the side pocket of his camel-coloured winterized trench coat. He greeted me with a quick handshake and a smile.

We entered the school, found the main office, and were ushered into the vice-principal's office, where a gangly man welcomed us and begged us to sit.

"Tragedy," he murmured, "such a tragedy," as he fished Jason Hargove's file from a pile on his desk. "Jason was well-liked by his teachers. He seemed like a good kid, you know? Kind, respectful, did his work. Never saw him down here until he had that fist fight earlier this year."

"Fight?" Crestwood asked.

"With another student. Something about a video game or something. You know how kids can be."

I nodded to show that I did. Know how kids could be, I mean. The VP's students were only a hair's breadth away from my own since the government had abolished grade thirteen. We were getting them younger at the university these days, and that meant getting them more immature. Parents calling to advocate for their "kidult" children past the age at which professors can legally engage in such transactions have become ingrained in the post-secondary teaching experience. The VP looked at me quizzingly as I nodded, as if I'd gotten a secret password wrong or something. "I teach at the U of T," I told him. He nodded and emitted an "Ah" sound as realization took hold.

"We'd like to question some of Jason's friends and classmates," Crestwood said, "and teachers, coaches, you know, anyone who might be able to shed some insight on the matter."

"Of course," the VP said. He cleared his throat and adjusted his tie.

"Let's start with the boy involved in the fight."

7

Crestwood took the official questioning of Jason's friends and acquaintances that might be deemed suspect, and he asked me to speak informally to the staff. This was SOP whenever Crestwood was concerned. He took the official highroad while I mulled about after scraps, hoping someone would toss me a bone. I began by questioning Jason's basketball coach, a petite brunette with a ruddy complexion that, if it were not for her staff ID card and the whistle in her mouth, would have blended seamlessly with her students. When she noticed me, she blew her whistle, barked commands to the players, and bounced the ball back into play.

I introduced myself, and we spoke about Jason's basketball prowess, how he took command of the court whenever the ball was in play, in direct opposition to his demeanour outside of the game, which was indicative of a shy loner. Outside of an episode in which Jason's team, the home team, was heckled so badly that some boys in the bleachers had to be expedited from the gym lest it escalate, Jason had never been involved in an altercation to her knowledge.

At that point, a basketball landed with a thud, not more than three feet from where we stood. The coach caught it on the rebound without missing a beat and hesitated only slightly before tossing it back to a young man, standing several yards from us, watching us from a distance. The boy—if you could still call him that—had a long mop of unkempt, wavy dark hair that looked as if it hadn't been washed in weeks, and a fully grown, shaggy goatee. He looked like he'd be more at home wearing a leather jacket and perched on a motorcycle than wearing blue satin knee-pants, a sleeveless shirt, and playing basketball in a high school gym. But what made him stand out even more to my mind, besides the clothes he wasn't wearing and the challenging expression, was the tattoo he wore on his left bicep.

"I want to speak to him," I told her as I nodded in the boy's direction, "the boy with the asp."

"Loo-*cas!*" the coach called and she blew her whistle.

At the coach's beckoning, Lucas followed me to the office. He took a seat once inside, which allowed me to meet with Crestwood and the VP alone. I caught them just as they were winding down their questioning of Jason's sparring partner. When they dismissed him, Crestwood stood in the VP's doorway, watching the boy leave. "Stefan Barton," he told me. "He *was* our prime suspect."

"Was?" I asked.

"No connections to the ROM. Other than sour grapes over the fight and suspension that followed, there's really no motive either."

We watched as Stefan left the office. As he approached Lucas, he held out his hand, fingers curled into a fist. "Death before dishonour, man," Stefan said.

Lucas raised his fist to meet Stefan's and they fist bumped. "Death before dishonour," he confirmed.

The VP poked his head out of his office door and motioned for Lucas to enter.

"Check out the tattoo," I told Crestwood before Lucas was within earshot.

"Nice tat," Crestwood told him as he passed in front of us on his way into the office.

Lucas pulled the skin on his shoulder tight and craned his neck so he could admire the tattoo. "Thanks, man."

"It's an asp, right?" I asked.

"It's a *cobra*, dude." I thought about informing him that an asp *is* a cobra—an *Egyptian* cobra—but thought better of it.

"Does it have a story?" Crestwood asked.

"Naw, it's just a thing, you know?" the boy, Lucas, Luke, Pressman said. "A bunch of us guys got brave and decided to do it one night. Someone dared someone else and before you know it, we all had it, you know?" Did I know how it felt to have art work permanently etched under my skin in response to peer pressure? I scratched at the skeleton on my chest in answer to his question.

At that point, the vice-principal herded us into his office and he and Crestwood continued their questioning. When asked about the "Death before dishonour" motto, he seemed briefly flabbergasted. It took him a moment to formulate his answer. "It's a tag-line, man. You know, something to say. To be different. Unique. People always look for something different to have a reason, but sometimes something just *is*, you know? It's just something to say." I looked at Crestwood as if to say, *Methinks he doth protest too much.* Why give something that meant nothing so much credence?

Crestwood nodded; message received.

A quarter of an hour later we were all pretty sure that, outside of the tattoo, our vic had no ties to the boy sitting in front of us.

The VP was on the verge of dismissing Luke when Crestwood's cell rang. He grabbed a notepad and pencil from the VP's desk and slammed it down on the table in front of where Luke was sitting. "The tat. I want the names of everyone that was with you the night you got it." He excused himself to take the call.

The VP and I eyed each other in between the scritch-scratch of Luke's pencil on the paper. When Crestwood returned, he perused Luke's list.

"What's this?" he asked.

"That's it: the list of guys."

"These aren't names," Crestwood said.

"They're aliases," he said plainly, as if his reply needed no further clarification.

Crestwood gave the boy the evil eye until he flinched.

"Look, man, I swear: that's all I know," Luke added, on the defensive.

Crestwood continued to stare. I swear I think I heard him growl.

"That was the first time we'd ever met. We play games online." Luke looked from Crestwood to the VP, to me, and then back to Crestwood. "We never use our real names." The boy's response had grown to almost frantic proportion.

The office grew silent for a moment. The VP ended the silence by dismissing Luke.

"That's it? I can go?" Luke asked.

"You know what they say, Mr. Pressman, That 'it ain't over till the fat lady sings'?" There was no recollection of ever having heard the idiom or any fathom of understanding what it might possibly mean in the boy's expression. "This opera's just getting started," Crestwood warned.

The Mummy Wore Combat Boots

He paused and then told him they'd meet again. It sounded like a threat.

"The vic's tat was a fake," Crestwood told me on our way out of the school, "painted on post-mortem."

"They branded him," I said. "Marked their territory. Counted coup."

"Keep in touch, Richardson," he said. I started to walk to my car. "Hey," Crestwood said, calling me back. When I turned he was holding out his fist. "Death before dishonour, dude," he said quietly.

I shook my head as I walked toward my car, musing at Crestwood's sense of humour, so dry, it might as well be mummified.

9

That night, I went online and googled 'toronto + natron' and turned up one likely hit: a small shop on Queen called "New Order" that catalogued natron and palm and cedar oils amongst their eclectic inventory, an unlikely cocktail of chemicals for the twenty-first century, to be sure.

"New Order" was a small store with a black sign above the door depicting a white skull at one end and kelly green marijuana leaves at the other. Bongs, hemp clothing, and wax candles shaped like skulls graced the front window. It was the kind of place we used to call a "head shop" in my day. The interior was under-lit and stank of incense. A row of T-shirts depicting subversive graphics, most with cleverly hidden swear words, hung from fish wire on hangers like laundry set out to dry, only centimetres below yellowing, industrial ceiling tiles. Inspirational posters cloaked the walls like wallpaper.

A twenty-something hippie-chick greeted me from behind the front counter. Her straw-coloured hair had been parted in the middle and hung in long braids. She wore mid-seventies, beatnik-style clothing that were no doubt

31

fashioned from hemp. She knew exactly what natron was. "People use it as a natural cleanser," she said. "We import it from The Netherlands."

"How do you sell it?" I asked.

"We sell it in bulk or mix it with herbs to make sachets." She tossed one on the glass counter in front of her. Square and covered in gingham, it was about the size of my palm.

"Do you sell a lot of these?"

"Enough of them to keep selling them, I guess."

"And in bulk? In terms of weight? How much do you sell?"

She shrugged her shoulders. "Not a lot, usually. We keep it for the regulars, mostly." She tossed the sachet back on the counter behind her. "Oh!" Her face seemed to light up. "There was this one guy? Asked if I'd get him a whole bunch of it."

"Do you remember when?" I asked.

"Twice in the last year."

"Who was he?" I tried to contain myself; I'd actually stumbled on a lead. "Do you have his name?"

She shook her head. "No, no name."

I sucked in a breath, ready to ask my next question, but she beat me to the punch.

"Paid cash. No need to get his name."

"What did he look like?"

"Tall guy. Thin and wiry. Reddish hair. Older guy. Balding. Looked like he'd lost more hair than he'd kept."

"Did you get anything else? Where he lived? Where he worked? Why he needed the natron?"

"Said he was a professor at the university."

"Did you get *which* university?"

32

"Toronto. U of T." Bingo! I thought, Right in my own backyard.

"Said he needed it for his Egyptology class and that they might mummify some animals or something. Morbid, yet strangely cool."

Did I say in my own backyard? Forget that—this was right under my roof. I knew who the man was: Clinton Johns, Professor of Archaeology and chronic pain in my butt. Clint and I used to be friends, but we'd had a falling out a few years back over semantics. We've maintained a professionally cordial but cool relationship ever since.

I thanked the girl for her help, took her card out of politeness, and left, still smelling the incense on my clothes in spite of the crisp winter air.

10

I caught Clinton Johns in his office later that afternoon. Clint's office was darker than most. He liked the shades drawn, said the light gave him a headache. A single desk lamp with a green, glass shade, one that might have been more at home on a banker's desk, was the sole source of illumination. I had to squint to read the features on his reedy face.

Yes, he'd purchased natron—a rather large quantity—on two occasions. The first time he'd used the chemical to mummify a number of small animals recently put down at the local humane society. Cats and dogs, mostly, supplemented with a few mice purchased at the local pet store.

The second time he'd brokered the purchase for someone else. "There was this one guy," Clint told me. "One of my old students. Said his cousin wanted it to mummify an animal for a school project. Had gotten the instructions off the 'Net."

"That's quite an awful lot of natron for a single animal. Did you ask him what kind?"

"He said there were going to be a few. I don't know...a mouse? Maybe a rabbit, he said. Why does it matter?"

"Because we think your guy used it to mummify a human being."

Clint drew a sharp breath in between his teeth like he was experiencing sudden, acute pain. "Shit," he said.

"What was his name?"

"The student or the cousin?" he asked. Clint put his feet up on his desk. I noticed the left sole of his tan cowboy boots was wearing thin.

"The cousin."

"Never asked." What do the kids say in this situation? "Burn"? "Psych"? He'd set me up for that one and I'd fallen, hook, line, and sinker.

"Clint," I said, surprised at how angry it sounded. I took a deep breath—in through the nose, out through the mouth—it had a calming effect.

"The student," I said, temperately.

"His name," he hesitated. He bit off the tip of his thumbnail, spit it onto the floor, and went to work on the adjacent finger. Clint's a reformed smoker. It was the cigarettes that mostly got him through tense times during our undergrad. "Omar!" he blurted. "No, no, that's not quite it. Oleg, maybe?"

This behaviour was typical of Clint. His memory was like a sieve for things that had no direct consequence for him. Students come and go each and every term. Professors quite frequently look out into a sea of hundreds of bodies. After a while, year in, year out, they begin to look amorphous. Faceless. Under ordinary circumstances I wouldn't have faulted him for the

36

lapse in memory, but he'd gone out of his way to get this guy what essentially amounted to a smoking gun. You'd think he'd remember something like that. What I couldn't figure out was whether Clint was being his usual, apathetic self or intentionally evasive, which was par for the course whenever I tried to have a conversation with him. "Can you describe him?"

"Young." So were most of the people on campus. "Pale complexion. Doughy body. His hair was dark, tinged with copper, you know? The boys do it to be different, but so many of them do it they all wind up looking the same. You've gotta love the irony." He righted himself in his chair and leaned on his elbows as he peered at me from the other side of the desk. Clint and used to be close once, tight, like brothers. Come to think of it, this was probably the most Clint and I had spoken since the break-up. I hated to admit it, but I missed the relationship.

"Stringy, his hair was. Like he hadn't washed it in days. Didn't talk much, either. Spoke in one word sentences or in grunts, like he didn't have the time for small talk, like he was better than small talk." Clint opened his desk drawer and brought out a package of gum, pulled out a stick, unwrapped it, and popped it into his mouth. "Want one?" he offered me as an afterthought.

He chewed thoughtfully for a moment. "Oliver!" he said. He snapped his fingers and pointed simultaneously. "His name. It was Oliver."

I knew who the kid was. Oliver Taft. Graduated last year, I think. "You wouldn't have gotten an address for him, would you?"

"Dude," was all he said. I remember reading once that the word "dude" had infinite connotations, each depending on the voice inflection and body language of the speaker. The way Clint had said it, it was fraught with incredulity, as if I'd just asked if he could spot me a million dollars until the next pay day.

I thanked Clint and resolved myself to looking up Taft's address in the department files.

11

Oliver Taft lived in the basement of his parents' semi, a hop, skip, and a jump north of the city. He had graduated near the bottom of his class with a minor in Anthropology. After unsuccessfully trying to convince me to hire him as an excavator on a site the department was sponsoring, he avoided me and my classes. According to his records, he took the majority of his classes from Clint, a few from my wife, and a smattering of others from an assortment of my staff. He seemed surprised to see me when showed up on his doorstep. He invited me in, offered me a soda, and we carried on a stilted conversation about how life had been treating him since he'd graduated.

Clint had been right—getting Taft to talk was like pulling teeth. From what I could put together, Taft was having difficulty finding his niche. After graduation, he'd expected to gain an entry-level job somewhere in the city and work his way up the corporate ladder. That was the dream; The reality saw Taft waiting tables at the neighbourhood Swiss Chalet, supplementing his income stocking shelves at the local Walmart overnight.

We spoke in his parents' living room. I asked him about the natron. He seemed wary at first, dodging the question as to where he'd gotten it until I assured him his beloved Professor Johns wouldn't get into trouble.

"Professor Johns had us do the mummification thing to some animals. Embalmed things, mostly. Like what they dissect in the science lab," Taft said. He laughed. "No one wanted to kill the things themselves." I got the feeling that Taft would've. Killed the animals, I mean. Without hesitation. Something about the way he'd said it, about the way he'd smiled when he'd said it, made me shudder. I took to studying the faces in the collection of family portraits perched on a high coffee table in the corner of the room to keep from thinking about it.

"I did a cat," Taft bragged. "One that wasn't embalmed. It was cool, you know? Watching the things dry up from day to day, cleaning them, wrapping them, and what not."

"You had so much fun you wanted to try it again. On your own," I suggested.

"What?" he asked, absent, distracted, as if he were Theseus lost in the labyrinth of his memories and my voice was the string that had guided him out.

"You purchased some natron from Professor Johns—"

"Oh, yeah. Yeah," he said, voice trailing off as he tried to remember. "No. The stuff wasn't for me. It was for my cousin."

"Do you have a name?" No sooner had I asked than my question was answered. I picked up the photo I'd been looking at, a portrait of an extended family. Blue-rinsed, bee-hived matriarch and balding, comb-overed patriarch, sitting next to each other in the centre, grinning, showing what little teeth they had left. An assortment of their children, some next to spouses, some alone, all surrounded by a gaggle of grandchildren and a spattering of great-grandchildren. For me, one of the grandchildren stood out, a boy of about seventeen, dressed in black, dark, greasy hair, unkempt beard, and peering out from beneath one of his t-shirt sleeves? The sanguine eyes of an emerald asp. I made the connection to the cousin about a fraction of a second before Taft spoke his name.

12

Michael Crestwood is a huge, bear of a man. He's nearly bald and wears a thick goatee, liberally sprinkled with grey. A beefy scar that traces the curve of his left eye is emphasized when he sneers, which he does often, giving him the aura of an evil genius. In spite of his appearance (or perhaps because of it), Crestwood is a master interrogator, adept at pulling a confession from the perpetrator of any crime. I've seen him in action often enough to know a couple of high school boys were no match for him; he'd have them talking in time for dinner.

I arrived at 52 Division, asked for Crestwood, and was directed toward a rather large crowd of officers. Further queries as to his whereabouts landed him square in the din. The prudent course of action was to have a seat nearby and wait for the swarm to subside.

Soon enough, the crowd parted, and a pair of EMTs hurriedly rolled someone wearing an oxygen mask out on a stretcher. The EMT bringing up the rear held an IV bag level with his shoulder.

It seemed even police constables slowed to see an accident.

Crestwood followed the last EMT—this one toting a portable defibrillator—through the cleave in the crowd. "What happened?" I asked him.

"Kid took one look at me and nearly shit himself." He chuckled. "Hyperventilated himself into one hell of an anxiety attack. Sweat so much you could sop it up with a sponge." His smile made me uncomfortable, like he was enjoying the situation way too much. "The kid blacks out, falls out of his chair, smashes his head on the floor—the *back* of his head, mind—and cracks it open. Blood *everywhere.* Now *that's* what I call poetic justice."

I looked back to the front entryway as I considered the urgent footsteps of the paramedics on their way out. "This Lucas Pressman we're talking about?" I asked.

Crestwood shook his head, still grinning. "The guy he gave up. The kid that *really* wanted the natron. Talk about a glass jaw."

"He going to be okay?" I asked.

"He'd better be. Natron-boy, Pressman, played it cool. Until I threatened to press charges, that is. Then he gave up his friend, Arturo Cantwell, the guy on the stretcher. Co-op student at the ROM. Do I need to say any more?" Crestwood clapped my shoulder twice in a show of camaraderie. "Come, let's get this over with. The guy in the hospital's the one I really want to see. If anyone's going to crack it's going to be him."

13

Crestwood barged into the interrogation room like a bull in a china shop. I followed him in with a slightly smaller profile. He jerked a chair out from under the table in the middle of the room with the scrape of a hundred fingers simultaneously scratching on at least as many chalkboards. It reverberated off the barren concrete block in the stark room. "So, Mr. Pressman," Crestwood addressed Luke as he dropped himself into the chair with a thud, "remember that fat lady we talked about the other day? Well, she's a singin'." Luke's expression clearly showed he still had no idea what on God's green earth Crestwood was talking about.

I covered my mouth to suppress a grin. I wondered how long Crestwood had been waiting to use that particular line.

There was a knock on the door and a uniformed officer brought in a tray of drinks. At some point, Crestwood had ordered the kid a Coke and coffees all around for the adults. The mother looked worn. Worried. Her complexion was mousy, her eyes, red and swollen. The dad sat straight-backed in the chair, arms crossed over his chest. I recognized him from Taft's portrait. His moustache was tinged with grey, his lips chapped. He began to speak the second Crestwood stopped, demanding to know why his son was being held. As far as he was concerned, we were compelled to lay our cards on the table or fold. I waited for Crestwood to respond while I contemplated my coffee cup.

Crestwood had said the kid was cool; he was downright cold. He stared at us through brown eyes exuding less life than a stale campfire. He had the physique of someone who ate too much junk food and got very little exercise. His complexion was ashen, his hair gathered into a loose ponytail at the nape of his neck. He was dressed in army fatigues from head to toe.

Dad hollered at Crestwood to check the boy's friends. The accusations against his son had no base. If the evidence had pointed to him—and it appeared to do so—it was because someone had made it seem that way.

Crestwood countered with the information he'd learned while interviewing people—the administration, teachers, and students—at his school. Luke Pressman was known as an introvert. He knew his way around the Internet and the law. His academic record was marred by a series of failed credits, drug busts, and suspensions for everything from threats against teachers to weapons possession. He hung out with a group of boys that couldn't find a clique to join, so they'd created their own. His friends were tight-lipped. They were a part of an online gaming community, a virtual brigade, where the rule was kill or be killed. They stuck together, like musketeers. They worshipped the first kid Crestwood had interrogated at the school, Stefan Barton, a leader in a cohort of followers. The way Crestwood had heard it, Stefan wore their allegiance like a badge or a bullet-proof vest. As long as the group remained loyal, Stefan was invincible.

"How did Jason fit into your group?" Crestwood asked.

"He didn't," Luke answered.

"What did you use the natron for?" I asked.

"Like I told you before: my cousin, Ollie, got it for me and I got it for Art," Luke said.

"That good for nothing son-of-a-bitch, Taft," the father growled. "Bastard just like his father." The photograph at the Tafts' had painted such a happy picture, multiple generations of a single family, tolerating the close proximity to one another during the shoot, smiles all around. It suddenly occurred to me that a picture could obscure a thousand more words than it spoke.

"And once more, just for Dr. Richardson: what did Art need it for?"

"I told you already: I don't know. He said he wanted it and—"

"And you went out of your way to get it out of the goodness of your heart."

"Enough, Luke," the father admonished, "say nothing more." To Crestwood, he demanded, "How do you know my Lucas had anything to do with this murder? My son says he knows nothing about it. Show me the evidence."

I'd had enough of their subterfuge. "Oh, we have the evidence," I blurted. "The evidence is buried in the mummy's casing. Do you know what cartonnage is? It's like papier mache: linen and plaster. It's like a cast: sticky when wet. Trace evidence gets embedded in the cartonnage—

fingerprints, skin cells, hair, clothing fibers—all there, waiting for us to find it."

Dad tried to stare me down for a moment. At last he uttered, "We want a lawyer."

Crestwood eyed me. His sarcastic grin begged, "What took them so long?"

14

Crestwood made a quick call to the principal of the school to fill in the blanks. Yes, Jason had shared classes with Stefan, although the two were not known to be friends. In fact, the two had gotten into an argument days before Jason's disappearance, the fight the VP had alluded to earlier. Neither boy had admitted to being the aggressor in the fight and they were both sentenced to an in-school suspension as a result.

He hung up with the principal, Crestwood did, and gave me the gist of the conversation.

"So what now?" I asked.

"The hospital," he said. "I want to question the other boy."

15

Arturo Cantwell, the hospitalized boy, seemed to have recouped some since we'd last seen him. Save for a large swath of bandages that covered the back of his head, you'd never know anything was wrong. His mother sat at his bedside. His father paced the room. A woman dressed in a suit the colour of Italian eggplant—unmistakably the lawyer—hovered in the far corner.

Crestwood made the introductions for both of us. The father shook our hands. "My son wants...he *needs*...to tell his story," he said.

At that point, the lawyer stepped forward. "I have, of course, advised my client to remain silent, but he's decided to refuse this advice and insists on speaking to you," she said to Crestwood. "I trust that when you discuss my client's case with the prosecutor for the Crown, you'll beg leniency for his involvement."

"That depends on what he has to say," Crestwood said. The attorney nodded at the boy.

"Okay. First of all, I need to say that I didn't do this. I was just helping out a friend. Trying to keep him out of trouble."

"Arturo," the father said, sternly.

"Okay, okay," he said as if annoyed. "My friends. We play *Commando Troop*."

"I know that game. I hear my students talk about it," I offered. "You play online, right? What is it? Combat? Mercenary for hire?"

"Yeah," Arturo, Art, confirmed. "Ex-soldiers. Anti-terrorists working as a covert team to take out enemies and terrorist cells. Stefan was our leader. There were four on our team: Stefan, me, and Lucas and another guy. We were among the top four scorers in the entire world. Dude! The *whole* world! Then Jason came along.

"He'd listen while we talked, discussing what we did online, bragging about successful missions, mostly. Pretty soon, Jason joined online and started rallying to join our team. Stefan made it brutally clear to him that he wasn't welcome to play with us. That's when Stefan made us get the tats. You know, all that semper fi shit."

Dad voiced his aversion to Art's language by clearing his throat.

"Within days, Jason had formed his own team and over the next few weeks, it started rising up the ranks. Then it got competitive. We'd have arguments—mostly Stefan and Jason—about which team was best. Then it spread to the 'Net—Jason's team seemed set on taking *us* out instead of the terrorists.

"They targeted us, started engaging us in combat."

"Online?" Crestwood asked.

Art nodded. "This one attack? They ambushed us. Stopped us from completing our mission. All of us were wounded. Cost us some serious HP."

"HP?" I asked.

"Health points.

"Stefan called Jason on it the next day at school and they got into it."

"The fist fight," said Crestwood. "The in-school suspension."

Art nodded. "A teacher had to break it up. Stefan probably would have killed Jason right then and there if he hadn't. To retaliate, Stefan told us to target Jason's team in the game."

"Just like that?" asked Crestwood. "What? He says, 'Jump,' and you ask, 'How high'?"

"Stefan was our squad leader. He out-ranked us. So when Stefan said, 'Target Jason's team', we targeted Jason's team. Trouble is, Jason made it personal. He sought out Stefan's character on a number of assaults. Engaged him in both hand-to-hand *and* weapons combat. He hunted Stefan down like an animal."

"You mean, 'he hunted Stefan's *character* down'," said Crestwood.

"He killed his character?" I asked.

Art nodded again.

"I don't get it," Crestwood said. "You were playing a game. *A game!* You get out, you restart the game. Jason killed Stefan's *character*. So what?"

"You don't understand," Art said, squirming to find a more comfortable position on the hospital bed. "We spend weeks, sometimes months, training the characters in a variety of combat situations before we get the missions. As you get better, you get more challenging missions. Stefan could have created another character, but it would have taken time to train him to the same status as the one Jason had killed. Stefan was devastated."

"It was a *character,*" Crestwood repeated.

"It was Stefan's alter-ego. As far as Stefan was concerned, when Jason killed his character, he killed a part of him."

"So you guys decided to *kill* him?" asked Crestwood.

"No! No. I already told you: I had nothing to do with it."

"Then tell me what did happen, then."

"That's just it: I don't know how it happened. I wasn't there. When I got there, Jason was already dead. He was lying on the floor in a pool of blood. Stefan was panicked. He told me Jason had fallen, that it had been an accident. I helped him get the body into his parents' freezer until we could figure out what to do with him."

"Come on," Crestwood said. "You expect me to believe the body was in his parents' deep freeze and they never found out?"

"Stefan's basement is unfinished, but he made himself a rec room down there anyway. It's his sanctuary. His parents respect his privacy." Art glared at his father as if to imply his parents weren't as understanding as Stefan's parents were. "They never go down there. If they need something out of the deep freeze, they holler down for Stefan to get it."

"Go on."

"That's it," Art said, confused. "I helped him clean up the blood and that's it."

"Where does the museum come into all of this?" I asked.

"The museum was a stroke of genius on Stefan's part." He sounded proud. "I was already doing co-op at the ROM. I'm working on a diorama for next month's Mummies Roadshow exhibit."

"So you just mummified him and snuck him into the museum?"

Art nodded. "I learned how to make a mummy online, and bought what we needed. We practiced on small animals first."

"Small animals?" Crestwood sounded squeamish.

"Yeah, like a rabbit and a cat. When we were ready, we did Jason, wrapped him up, and painted it so it'd look authentic."

"But how did you get him into the museum?" I wondered.

"That was easy. We told security it was a fake for our exhibit. They knew me because I used to talk them up when I was there. It was Stefan's idea to bring him along and introduce him to the guards a few days before we brought Jason in. Worked like a charm."

Once more the father cleared his throat. Art continued in a lower key. "Once we were in the museum, we put it in storage with some other mummies."

"Where you figured it would stay with all the other forgotten artifacts," I said.

Art nodded. "We didn't plan on them having to move the storage room during renovations."

"And the tattoo? Why give him the tattoo?"

"Stefan's idea again. Said Jason would've wanted it that way, to finally be a part of the group, like we were honouring him in his death by giving what we didn't while he was alive. Stefan said it's what the ancient Egyptians would've done."

"And that's the whole story, gentlemen. Do you think you could get us a deal?" the lawyer asked.

"I'll have to speak with the Crown attorney, but I don't know. Your client was a willing participant in a brutal murder over nothing more than a video game, even if it was after the fact," Crestwood said.

"This was *not* over a video game," Art insisted. "When Jason killed Stefan's character, he killed part of Stefan, too. What Stefan did? It wasn't murder; it was retribution."

I tried to imagine a world in which health points and pixels mattered more than flesh and bone, a world where the virtual was more real than the real itself, but my mind couldn't fathom it. The full weight of Art's words seemed to sink slowly into Crestwood's psyche. When the last had reached full absorption, Crestwood stood and walked to the door behind him. I followed. He rapped twice. A uniformed officer opened the door.

"Stefan Barton. Bring him in," Crestwood told him. "Charge the other two as accessories."

I watched as a second constable handcuffed Art's wrist to the bed frame. From his shirt pocket, the officer withdrew a card and read Art his rights.

"Dr. Richardson?" Crestwood said, extending a hand. "Always a pleasure."

"Detective Crestwood," I said, shaking it. Crestwood walked in the direction of the elevators and I followed him. We nodded at each other as we entered the elevator and traversed the distance in awkward silence.

As we parted ways outside of the hospital, it struck me as somehow funny this case had ended as it had begun, here, in this downtown hospital, a stone's throw from both the museum and my office. I checked my watch. If I hurried, I could just make it to pick my wife up after her last class and be home in time for dinner.

THE FURTHER ADVENTURES OF PALMER RICHARDSON IN...

THE NEXUS

AND OTHER STORIES

Aliens, ghosts, the paranormal, a glimpse at a possible future...

There are more things in heaven and earth than modern man will ever know or understand.

The Nexus

They say be careful what you wish for. Meet Josef Schliemann, noted expert in pseudo-archaeology who sponsors a dig beneath a historic church in downtown Toronto. Said to have been built on a tract of land sacred to prehistoric Indigenous peoples living the in the area the secrets of the site have been lost to time. Will Josef survive when he finds the object of his desire?

A Morgan by Any Other Name

In a future where cloning has been perfected—sort of—Rachel, a Morgan model, should have the world at her feet, but she's not happy. What is the one thing a teenage clone desires?

At the Mere Thought Of
What happens when your worst nightmare comes true? Businessman Crane is about to find out.

The Circle of Life
Bob wakes up the night after attending a wild rave to find he's not himself. He wakes up, buried alive, and hungry...for flesh.

One book, thirteen stories.

In The Nexus and Other Stories, science fiction author Elise Abram explores the myths of the modern world.

THE FURTHER ADVENTURES OF MOLLY McBRIDE AND PALMER RICHARDSON IN...

PHASE SHIFT

If you knew the world was about to end, what would you do?

If you found the key to another Earth, would you use it?

When archaeologist Molly McBride finds the key to a doppelganger Earth she is swept into a world of conspiracy that could end in the death of not one, but two planets.

Will Molly be able to prevent the impending cataclysm?

THROWAWAY CHILD

A recent report written after a six-year investigation into residential schools for Canadian First Nations people stated that at least 3,201 student deaths occurred in these schools, with many more going unrecorded.

The report goes on to state that "many students who went to residential school never returned. They were lost to their families...No one took care to count how many died or to record where they were buried."

Prime Minister Justin Trudeau, in a 2016 speech to the Assembly of First Nations Special Chiefs Assembly said, "We know all too well how residential schools and other decisions by governments were used as a deliberate tool to eliminate Indigenous languages and cultures."

Throwaway Child

is the story of one of these children.

The skeleton of a young girl is found beneath the cement basement floor in an abandoned Victorian in Toronto. On duty is Detective Constable Michael Crestwood who contacts forensic anthropologist Dr. Palmer Richardson to assist in the investigation. What they uncover is the story of a six-year-old Cree girl, stolen from her family, warehoused in a government run facility and then forgotten.

In a story with ties to current headlines, THROWAWAY CHILD explores the injustice experienced by two girls imprisoned in a mid-twentieth century residential school, their families, and the tragedy that results from one girl's need to find a home.

www.ingramcontent.com/pod-product-compliance
Lightning Source LLC
Chambersburg PA
CBHW071210130626

46555CB00004B/1656